Dedicated to:
My dearly loved sons, Jakey and Theo.
Reach for the stars and follow your dreams,
but above all else - continue to shine and be kind. x

With special thanks to:
My wonderful Mom and Dad, Georgie and Pete.
For your endless love, unwavering belief
and continuous support.

-N.P.

For Ana and Estella. May your kindness, silliness,
and sweetness always shine bright.

-N.M.

First published in 2018.
Sea School Stories, Staffordshire, England.

© 2018 Natalie Pritchard

A CIP catalogue record for this book is available from the British Library.

MONTY the MANATEE

Words by
NATALIE PRITCHARD

Pictures by
NATALIE MERHEB

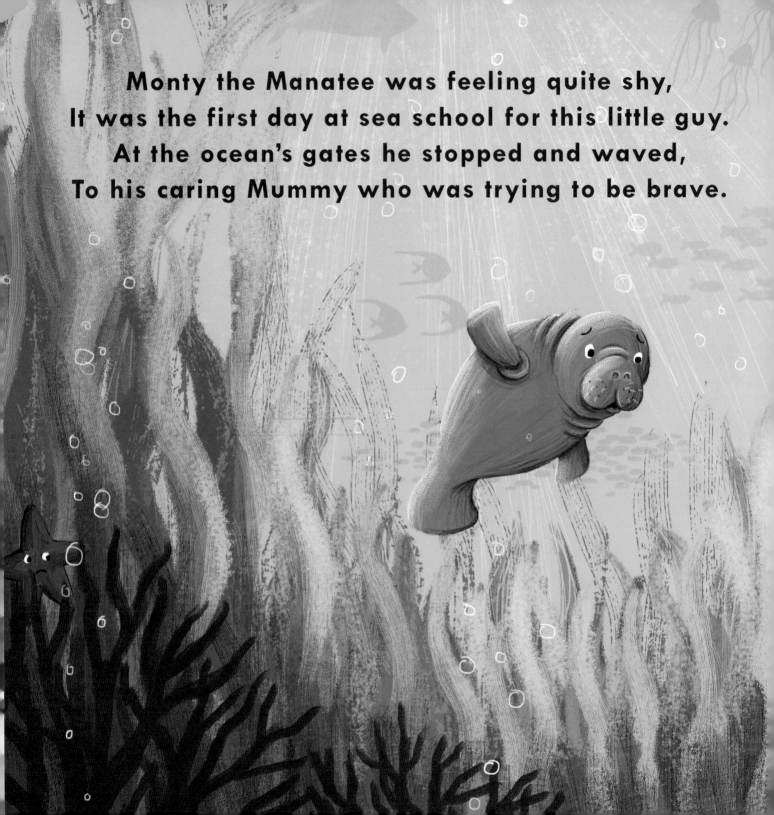

Monty the Manatee was feeling quite shy,
It was the first day at sea school for this little guy.
At the ocean's gates he stopped and waved,
To his caring Mummy who was trying to be brave.

"You'll be mighty fine son, now off you go."
So Monty paddled his chubby flippers
really, really slow.

Some jellyfish were chatting in the sea grass,
So he bravely swam up to them and politely asked:
"My name's Monty, would you please play with me?
"It's my very first day at this school in the sea."

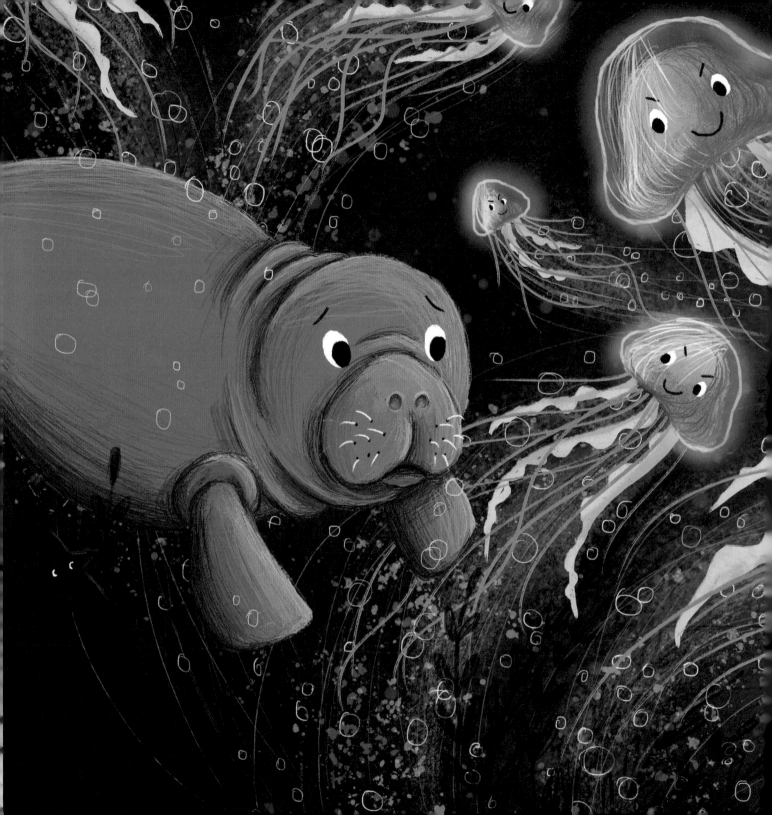

The jellyfish whooshed their tentacles in disgust,
"Leave us alone, this is a private chat, SHUSH!"

In the classroom, Monty met Sidney the shrimp,
Who held up his fists and shouted: "You're a WIMP!"
Monty said sorry, he didn't mean to offend,
He just wanted someone to be his friend.

At lunchtime, Sammy seal
was eating a small fish,
So Monty offered him something
from his very own dish.
The seal wasn't interested
in Monty's friendship or food,
"I like fast and cool creatures.
Leave me alone dude!"

A school of fish who
were swimming nearby,
Thought it would be funny
to join in, so they cried:

"Who wants to be mates with a manatee?
The ugliest creatures in the sea!
They're slow and clumsy most of the time,
There's NO WAY you can be a friend of mine!!"

Suddenly the sea creatures stopped and froze,
They saw a dark shadow beneath the mangroves.

A huge shark raced at them,
with jaws stretched wide, yelling:
"YOU'RE FOR MY SUPPER,
SO DON'T TRY TO HIDE!"

Clever Monty knew how he could make the shark STOP,
By closing his eyes he resembled a rock!
So he tucked all his friends under his tummy,
Staying completely still, as taught by his Mummy.

They all held their breath as the shark swam near,
The jellyfish and seal were quivering with fear!

PHEW!! Monty's trick had finally worked...
'The shark thought I was a rock!" he smirked.

Monty's school friends gave him a great big cheer,
"HOORAY FOR MONTY, HE HAS NO FEAR!"
They were sorry for treating him badly before,
And they realised now that he wasn't a bore.

Monty agreed that they should all be friends,
He just wanted the awful bullying to end.
So the creatures played nicely from that day on,
And Monty passed on this message to everyone:

"Slower, faster,
thinner or fatter;
It's what's on the inside
that really matters.
Just think about
the hurt you might cause,
when you tell someone
they can't play anymore.

If you look around
I think you will find,
The world is a better place
when we all

BE KIND."

FACTS ABOUT MANATEES

Did you know......?

• **Manatees live mainly in shallow waters in the Gulf of Mexico, Caribbean Sea, Amazon Basin and West Africa.**

• **They are gentle, slow creatures and are sometimes known as sea cows.**

• **Adult manatees can grow up to around 4 metres long (as long as a car!) and can weigh over 450 kilograms.**

• **Manatees are mammals, which means they cannot breathe underwater and usually come up for air every 3 or 4 minutes. However, they can hold their breath for up to 20 minutes.**

• **They mostly eat plants and algae, but sometimes eat small fish.**

• **Manatees are intelligent, like dolphins, and can communicate with each other by making chirping, squeaking and whistling sounds.**

• **Manatees can live to be up to 60 years old and they are a protected species under the Marine Mammal Protection Act.**

SEA SCHOOL STORIES

Monty the Manatee is the first book in a fun and educational series, called Sea School Stories, which aims to encourage emotional intelligence in children by helping them to flourish in this challenging world. The books cover different topics, all based on our loveable Sea School characters, and teach key qualities such as kindness, empathy, social skills, self-control, dealing with emotions and handling relationships.

To order a copy of Monty the Manatee and to keep up to date with the latest news and updates from Sea School Stories visit:

WWW.SEASCHOOLSTORIES.CO.UK

 Follow us on instagram

@seaschoolstories and @authornataliepritchard

The next book from Sea School Stories will be published in 2019.

Be Kind Always x

Printed in Great Britain
by Amazon